When the World Stopped

by Anne Schraff

Perfection Learning® Corporation
Logan, Iowa 51546

Cover Design: Mark Hagenberg

Cover Image Credit: Taxi (Rights-managed)

For information, contact:
Perfection Learning® Corporation
1000 North Second Avenue, P.O. Box 500,
Logan, Iowa 51546-0500.
Phone: 1-800-831-4190 • Fax: 1-800-543-2745
perfectionlearning.com

PB ISBN-10: 0-7891-6661-5 ISBN-13: 978-0-7891-6661-6
RLB ISBN-10: 0-7569-4760-x ISBN-13: 978-0-7569-4760-6

2 3 4 5 6 7 PP 15 14 13 12 11 10
PPI / 02 / 10

1

"YOU'RE SO QUIET, Mark," mocha-skinned Sharee Parks complained during lunchtime at Bunche High School.

Mark smiled, grateful that a sweet, pretty girl like Sharee even bothered with him. Mark was terrible at making conversation. He marveled at guys who could just ramble on about everything. "Yeah," he said.

"What are you thinking about? The test tomorrow?" Sharee tried to draw him out.

"I guess," Mark said. But it wasn't that. It was never about tests or school. It was the secret Mark Ryder couldn't talk about. The secret that burned a constant flame within his heart and soul.

"You'll do fine on the test," Sharee said. "Don't worry about it. What good does worry do, anyway?" She laughed. She had a warm tinkling laugh, like a delicate wind chime hanging from a tree branch. Sharee had a laugh like Mark's mother.

Even though Mark's mother had died 12 years ago, he still remembered her laugh. He remembered the big Victorian house where they lived, with the jacaranda tree out front. When he was a little boy it used to drop blue blossoms all over the lawn, and his mom would playfully put them on his head.

"So how's your dad doing?" Sharee asked. Mark had told her that his father was recently promoted at the biotech firm where he worked as a chemist.

"He's okay," Mark said.

"You guys aren't very close, huh?" Sharee asked. Her own father was a big, burly bear of a man who roared with laughter and delighted in all his children.

"I guess not," Mark admitted. That was putting it mildly, though.

Mark was afraid of his father, although Harry Ryder had never hit him or even yelled at Mark in a furious way. Mr. Ryder was an intense, soft-spoken man who rarely smiled.

"Mark, you and I need to do something fun this weekend. Let's go to the splash park. Everybody is talking about how fun it is," Sharee said.

"Maybe," Mark said. He was glad when the bell rang for class. He cared a lot for Sharee, but he wasn't comfortable with her. He knew she was frustrated that he didn't talk more. He sometimes wished that she could just be with him and not expect conversation.

Mark walked slowly toward English class. He thought of *that night* again, just like he did every day. It was the night his world stopped. Mark was four years old, and he had been in bed for a while. He had suddenly been awakened by yelling and screaming from downstairs—like he had never heard before. He burst into frightened tears. His father's thin, soft voice had been stretched into harsh, abrasive tones that made him sound like a strange ogre. It didn't even sound like his dad's voice. His mom was screaming and yelling too.

Mark had no idea what was going on. He had never heard his parents acting like this before. He dove under the covers of his bed, burrowing like an animal in a frantic effort to make the terrible sounds go away.

Then there was a thumping sound, something falling down the stairs, hitting every step. All the screaming and yelling stopped abruptly. It was as if Mark had been watching a wild, noisy television show, and suddenly it had been turned off. But the silence did not last long. Soon there were sirens, and the clumping of strange feet and unfamiliar voices. Mark shivered in his bed, even though it was springtime.

Now Mark walked into English class, trembling with the memory again. He sat down, trying to shake the memory away. But he couldn't. It stuck in his brain like glue.

Mark remembered his grandparents coming upstairs. His grandma was red-eyed from crying. His grandpa looked grim. His grandma kept saying over and over that everything would be all right. But her voice was forlorn and shaken.

After that, there was more confusion, more change. Mark went to live with his grandparents. He vaguely remembered going to his mother's funeral, putting a flower on her casket, seeing his father standing there like a ghost.

Little by little, Mark got used to living at his grandparents' house. His grandma was sweet and loving like his mom had been. His grandpa was funny and playful like his dad never was. Mark's dad came regularly to visit, but Mark never liked to be with him. Even back then he was afraid of him. Mark was always glad when his dad left.

When Mark was eight, he went back to live with his father. It wasn't what Mark wanted, but his dad had said it was time. His dad said a boy needed to be with his dad, and so it was.

Mark was deep in thoughts of the past when his English teacher, Mr. Larkspur, said, "I hope everybody is familiar with the Eudora Welty story."

Mark had read the story "A Visit of Charity," a bitter tale about a girl visiting some horrible old folks' home. Mark didn't like the story. He didn't like English either. He liked math and science. He had always dreamed about being an astronomer or having some job where he wouldn't have to mingle with people. He thought it would be nice to sit in an observatory and look for new planets. Planets and stars did not expect people to talk to them.

"Mark," Mr. Larkspur's voice came like an alarm, rousing Mark from his thoughts. "In what way might this be called a mirror story?"

"Uh, it's like real life," Mark said. "The girl hated the old women, and the nurse was cold. It's all real life. It's a horror story because life is horrible."

There was a funny silence in the room. Everybody seemed to be staring at Mark.

One girl, Brit Walsh, said, "I don't agree with Mark. I think the little girl in the story was really trying to be nice. It's a story about kindness."

"Actually," Mr. Larkspur said dryly, "Mark was pretty much on target. Yet, your philosophical comment was pretty dismal, Mark. Do you really think life is horrible?"

Yes, Mark thought to himself, because he remembered being four and playing in the sunshine with his mother under the jacaranda tree. The next day she was gone. Mark forced a smile and said, "No, I don't really feel like that."

Mr. Larkspur seemed relieved.

....

After school, Mark and Sharee walked across the street to get root beer floats. They sat in a booth sipping their sodas quietly.

As usual, Sharee began the conversation. "I ran into Brit Walsh on the way to meet you. She said that during English class you announced that life is horrible. Mark, that makes me feel so sad. Is life really horrible for you?" Sharee looked worried. Her beautiful brown eyes were filled with pity.

Mark thought Brit had a big mouth. She couldn't keep anything to herself. To Sharee, he said, "Oh, I didn't mean that. It was just something I said off the top of my head."

"Well, when people say things like that they're depressed. You do seem sad most of the time, Mark. I just wish you'd laugh more. I wish I could find a way to get through to you . . . " Sharee said.

It occurred to Mark that maybe the reason Sharee bothered with him was because she was one of those strange people who is attracted to miserable people like him. They see themselves as rescuers of lost souls, as lifeguards keeping sad spirits afloat, instead of letting them drown in their own misery. Maybe, Mark thought sadly, I'm more Sharee's patient than her friend.

"Sharee," Mark said, "you have to say something about those stupid stories we have to read. I hate them all, but Larkspur expects you to say something. So I did. It didn't mean anything."

"Let's go to the splash park on Saturday," Sharee said, with more urgency than usual. "I think it'd be great for . . . for both of us."

"Yeah, I probably can go," Mark said absentmindedly. His mind wasn't really focused on sun, water, or girls in bikinis. He was still thinking about his secret.

Mark had asked about the terrible night that his mother died long ago. His father and his grandparents had given him the same story. His mom had been home alone with him and somehow slipped at the top of the stairs and had fallen down the stairs headfirst. During the fall her neck had broken and she died.

Mark had never told anybody, not his father or his grandparents, about what he had heard that night. The terrible, screaming quarrel just before his mother fell to her death. The violent fight . . .

Sometimes Mark thought, or even hoped, that there had been no fight, and it was all a nightmare. That the fight was in his own bad dream, and his mom had fallen to her death in a simple, tragic accident. But then he would break into a cold sweat and realize that it had really happened. The fight and her violent death, one after the other. One *because* of the other? Had his dad pushed his mom? Had he thrown her or made her fall? *Had he killed her?*

2 MARK AND HIS FATHER lived four blocks from Bunche High School in a two-bedroom apartment.

Mark's dad had always put in a lot of overtime at work, but now with his promotion, he was able to do some work at his home computer. His dad was often there when he got home from school.

Mark wondered why his father never dated after his mom died. There were a lot of attractive women in Mr. Ryder's company, and he was a decent-looking man. He had an excellent job. Mark's dad was only 38, and he was young enough to start a new life. Mark wondered about it, but he never brought the subject up.

"Hey, Dad," Mark called out as he came in the door.

"Hello, Mark," his dad responded, pausing only briefly from his work. He never asked Mark how school was going.

Mark passed the living room and

paused a moment, staring at his father's back. He had wide shoulders and short, jet-black hair with no sign of thinning or graying. He was dark-skinned, more so than Mark's mom had been.

His dad had kept just one family picture in the living room, the one taken on Mark's second birthday. His mom, his dad, and little Mark. Such a happy family.

Mark remained standing there, his breath coming in heavy sighs. Why didn't he just ask his father? Why didn't he say, "Dad, something has been eating at me for all these years . . . that horrible fight I heard the night Mom died. You said you got home and found her dead, or dying or something, but what about before? I heard you guys fighting before she fell . . . what really happened?"

But it was impossible to even imagine asking such a question.

His dad suddenly turned from the glowing computer, seeing his son standing there. "What?" he asked, looking puzzled.

"Uh . . . nothing," Mark said. "I was just trying to remember what I was going to do . . . "

"Oh," his dad said, returning to the computer.

....

On Friday afternoon, as Mark walked home from school, Brit joined him. "Mark, I just found out last night that your mom and mine were in the same graduating class at Lincoln High," she said. "My mom was looking in her old yearbook and she said, 'Here's Belle Lee Crosley . . . she married Harry Ryder.' I've got the yearbook right here."

"Oh, yeah?" Mark said.

"Yeah, my mom told me your mom was the most popular girl in their class. She was really pretty. Look, here's one of her pictures," Brit said.

"Yeah, she was pretty," Mark agreed.

"My mom said all the kids who went to school with her felt really bad when she died. She was the first person from their class to die. She was only like 23 or something. You must have been just a baby," Brit continued.

Mark tried to pull away from Brit. He started hurrying down the sidewalk but she kept pace. "My mom said that she fell or something. How tragic. It must have been terrible for you," Brit went on in her dramatic voice.

"I don't remember much," Mark lied.

"Oh, that's good. You wouldn't want to remember stuff like that. Is your dad remarried? I mean, he must have been a really young widower," Brit said.

Mark considered crossing the street to get away from her. But he knew she'd just follow him across. "Uh, no, he's single," he muttered. "Hey, would you mind if I borrowed that yearbook? I'd like to look at all of it."

"Yeah, sure. Keep it for as long as you want," Brit replied.

"Well, see you, and thanks," Mark said, finally escaping her. He looked back once, relieved that she had turned a corner. Brit loved to gossip. Tomorrow she would be telling everyone the tragic thing that had happened to Mark's mother.

....

Mark and Sharee went to the splash park on Saturday. Mark enjoyed getting wet because it was a very warm day. He didn't have as much fun as Sharee did, but he pretended he did for her sake. After they dried off, they walked to the snack bar for corn dogs.

"Mark, you know everything about me, and I hardly know anything about you," Sharee began. "We've been in school together for ages! But you never share anything with me about yourself. Friends are supposed to share stuff."

"I like your new haircut," Mark said.

Sharee giggled. "That's not the kind of sharing I was talking about!" Then she turned serious. "I didn't even know that your mom died when you were a baby."

"Brit must have gotten on the phone last night," Mark groaned.

"Well, so what? She didn't say anything bad. She said your mom was homecoming queen at Lincoln High. That is so exciting. She said your mom looked like a movie star. I guess that's why you're so good-looking," Sharee said.

Mark felt his face turning warm. How could Sharee think he was good-looking? He was on the skinny side, and he didn't think his features were all that special either. His nose was too wide. He wasn't ugly or anything, but he didn't consider himself good-looking. He didn't know what to do, so he cast Sharee a lame smile and ate another bite of his corn dog.

"Mark, what happened to your mom?" Sharee finally asked.

"She, uh . . . died in a fall at home," Mark said. "I just wish Brit would mind her own business."

Sharee looked hurt. "When you care about somebody you want them to share their life with you. Don't you trust me enough to talk to me from the heart?" she asked.

"I'm sorry. Uh . . . see, we lived in this big Victorian house, and my mom fell down the stairs. Tripped on the rug or something. Uh . . . I heard her . . . fall . . . and I . . . uh . . . never saw her again . . . you know, alive," Mark said.

Sharee's eyes widened, and she looked stricken. "Oh, Mark, I'm sorry. It was stupid of me to pry. I just didn't think you still felt bad about it. I mean, I was about three when my grandma died, and I don't feel bad about it anymore. I'm really sorry I made you sad again . . . " she said.

Mark looked at the girl. He didn't know how to explain it. It was true that he was too young when it all happened to still be grieving now. He hardly knew what struck him when it actually happened. It wasn't grief that was tearing him up now, though. It was the question in his mind and heart. What had really happened that bitter night?

"It's okay, Sharee. Hey, let's go back in the water again," Mark said softly.

....

On Sunday, Mark rode his bike over to the neighborhood where he used to live. Mark had been there only one other time since his mom had died. Mark remembered his grandma looking for the jacaranda tree. His grandma smiled when she saw the tree. *Look at that, honey,* she had said to Mark, *your mama's blue tree. How she loved that tree. She used to say it rained pieces of the sky in the spring. Look how pretty it still is. Lordy, look at it.* She turned and smiled at Mark and asked, *You don't even remember it, do you, honey?*

Mark had nodded. Yes, he remembered the tree. He remembered sitting on the grass with his mother and playing there. He remembered it was the last happy place for him.

Now Mark started down the surprisingly familiar street, a lump in his throat, not sure why he was even doing this. He wanted to know the truth about that night 12 years ago, but he didn't expect to find it here on the street. He just had so many questions, so many dark corners in his mind . . .

As Mark neared the house, he was surprised to see the jacaranda tree in full bloom and the old Victorian home in excellent repair. Mark stood there for a moment, overcome with emotion. He looked up into the awesome branches of the tree. A few blue flowers fluttered gently down.

"Pretty, eh?" said a dry, crackly voice. It came from an elderly man with white hair. He smiled at Mark and said, "That tree was the reason my wife and I bought the house. She fell in love with the tree. Otherwise we would have passed the place up. The house stood empty almost a year before we took it. A terrible thing happened in the house, you know, and it spooked folks who were looking to buy it."

Mark turned numb at the man's words.

3 "YOUNG PEOPLE were living here," the old man continued, eager to tell his story. "The wife fell down the stairs and broke her neck. The neighbors who lived here at the time told us all about it. It was pretty awful."

"Oh," Mark said. His mouth was dry, and his skin felt clammy.

"Yep, according to the Kennerlys, the neighbors, the husband was an odd duck. Real quiet. Some kind of scientist. Everybody liked the wife. Lovely little gal. There were some nasty rumors around the time of the accident. Some folks thought the husband pushed the wife," the old man said.

Mark's mouth was so dry he thought he wouldn't be able to swallow if his life depended on it. "The police must have come and investigated and everything," Mark finally said.

"Sure, the police came," the old man said, "but in the end I guess they couldn't prove anything against the husband. Nobody was arrested. Mrs. Kennerly felt really bad about what happened to that young woman. She had a little boy, a toddler, I guess. Mrs. Kennerly went to the woman's funeral because, you know, they were neighbors. It was the least she could do. There was this poor little fellow, so bewildered. He went and put a flower on his mother's casket. Isn't that the saddest thing? Mrs. Kennerly said the little fellow didn't seem to know what was going on." The old man shook his head.

Mark didn't say anything. He just stood there looking at the man.

"Boy, you've got an awful sad look on your face. Did you know the woman who died here?"

"I just came to look at the tree," Mark mumbled, "the jacaranda tree. I, uh . . . saw it from a distance, and I wanted a closer look."

Mark glanced a last time at the jacaranda, then he turned and rode back down the street.

The man's words burned into Mark's already troubled soul. He was sorry he had come here. He was sorry he heard what the man had to say about his father. It just made things harder. It added more fuel to the fire of Mark's suspicions.

Mark could not imagine his even-tempered, quiet father exploding into such rage as he did that night. Something dreadful must have driven him over the edge.

But what could have started that terrible argument between Mark's parents? Mark was too young to know if there were serious problems in the marriage. Nobody knows such things when they are only four years old. All he knew was that his parents had never fought like that before. Something enormous must have happened to trigger the outburst.

Mark could not remember his father's activities that day. According to his father's story, he was working late and came home to find his wife on the floor at the bottom of the stairs. But of course, Mark knew that was a lie. It had to be a lie. Mark had heard a man's voice arguing with his mother.

Mark's head ached as he rode his bike toward home. The secret he was keeping was taking a toll on his body. He had to talk to someone. Anyone. And then suddenly it hit him. Mark wanted to find out more about his dad, so why not talk to his dad's dad? He was still alive, and in fact, he was in town for the next two weeks. He worked as a jazz pianist and traveled the country.

Mark headed toward town. What the man had said confirmed Mark's worst fears. It turned out that Mark wasn't the only one who suspected foul play in his mom's death.

Mark parked his bike outside the Green Onion, and he heard plunking on the piano as he walked in. It was murky inside the place, but he spotted the wiry old man's white head at the piano.

"Hi," Mark said as he neared his grandfather.

Moses Ryder squinted. "Mark?" he said like he wasn't sure. He was a fairly old man, and he looked it. The hard life of a traveling musician had wreaked havoc on the man's body.

"Yeah," Mark said. The last time Mark had visited his grandfather, he had referred to him as 'grandfather,' but he was corrected. "No, don't call me that," his grandfather had said at the time. "Everybody calls me Moe and you can too, boy."

"What's up?" Moe asked.

"You busy?" Mark asked.

"No, just warming up the fingers. I start playing when the customers come in, after 7:00 usually," he said. "So what's coming down? They haven't kicked you out of school, have they?"

"No. School's okay," Mark said.

"Want some brew? You like coffee, don't you?" Moses said, chuckling a little. "I live on coffee. It keeps my engine going. Black coffee, no cream or sugar. I like it thick as motor oil, dirty motor oil." He poured two cups, one for himself, one for Mark.

Mark felt awkward. He was sure he wanted to come here, but now he didn't know what to say. He wanted to come right out and ask his grandfather if his son, Mark's dad, was capable of making his wife fall that night. But Mark couldn't form the words.

Mark sat down in one of the chairs near the piano and drank the coffee. It was the worst coffee he had ever tasted. Moe grinned when Mark made a face. "Gonna make the hair stand up on the nape of your neck, boy," he said.

"I, uh . . . just wanted to ask you . . . uh . . . it's hard for me to get close to my dad. He's pretty quiet and, you know, I wondered if you'd know how I could . . . " Mark groped for words.

The old piano player laughed. "Harry never had much to say. I wouldn't fault him for it. He's got a first-rate mind. He's a crackerjack in that chemistry lab. The mad scientist, you know. You're the same, right, boy? You're one of those clams too," Moe said with a smirk on his face. "Only time I ever saw your dad open up was when something really angered him."

Moe must've seen the puzzlement on Mark's face, because he continued.

"He turns into somebody else," Moe said. "Have you ever seen your daddy angry?"

"No," Mark replied.

"Tell you what boy, just take him as he is. Don't try to have him be somebody else. How old are you now?" Moe asked.

"Sixteen," Mark said.

"Couple more years, you'll be out of there anyway. I've been on my own since I was 13." Moe laughed and then coughed.

Mark was unwilling to go. He had to try for more information. He longed for some clue that would reassure him that his father couldn't have harmed his mother. All Moe had done so far was make things worse.

"Did you like my mom?" Mark asked bluntly.

Moe blinked. "*Like* her? What kind of a question is that, boy? I hardly knew the woman. I met her after she and your daddy got hitched. I was on the road all the time in those days. Mark, what's going on? What's up?"

"I just was wondering about things . . . like how it was with my parents. I didn't have much time with Mom," Mark said.

"Well, Belle Lee was one good-looking girl. I saw that right away. I had a wife once, and I've seen plenty of girls, but your daddy married a looker. Woman like that draws more attention from guys than a blueberry pie draws flies." Mark's grandfather had a funny look on his face. "I asked your daddy if he was man enough for that much woman . . . "

"My mom and dad loved each other a lot, I guess," Mark said, fishing for information.

"He loved her. Man, he loved her. Look what he's turned into without her. A dried-up old man who isn't even 40. He loved your mama more than I could ever love a woman."

"My mom loved my dad too, though," Mark said.

Moses Ryder chuckled, an evil glint in his eyes. "Belle Lee loved your daddy as much as a pretty woman can love one man. That's all I'm going to say about that. Now I've got to crank up the music. Folks will be coming in soon."

Is that what they fought about that night? Mark felt chills go up his spine. Had his mom flirted with somebody? Or had some guy flirted with her and caused his dad to have a wild burst of jealousy? Is that what the terrible fight was about?

What had been a few wispy clouds floating in Mark's mind were quickly gathering into threatening storm clouds shutting out all the light.

"It's all in the past, boy," Moe said. "Don't be brooding about what happened years ago. It's done and can't be undone." He took another great gulp of black coffee. "Your mama was all right. But she wasn't any angel, you hear what I'm saying? None of us are angels. We're just people. She was all right, your mama, but she was no angel . . . "

4 MARK LEFT THE GREEN Onion with a heavier heart than he had brought in. It had all gone wrong. Moe had not reassured him. Instead, he had provided a motive for his dad's rage. Now Mark feared his mom had been flirting, or had seemed to be flirting, and that was enough to set his dad off.

Mark would have known nothing about the flirting. Mark's grandparents loved their daughter, and they would not have seen her faults clearly. Of course, they had never suggested to Mark that she was anything but a perfect, loving mom and a good wife. And that was the person Mark remembered too. They all wanted to believe in that picture on the mantel—his mom, his dad, and Mark, the happy, perfect, loving family. Mark wanted to believe in it too. The trouble was, he didn't anymore.

....

On Monday, as lunchtime neared, Mark looked for Sharee with special urgency.

He really needed her today. He didn't want to eat alone, not today of all days. If he had to eat alone he'd spend the whole time thinking about it.

But today, Mark did not see Sharee. He went into the cafeteria, picked up a tray and moved down the line, taking the day's special—turkey, mashed potatoes, and green beans. He kept glancing around, looking for the girl. He found a table and sat down. Maybe she was delayed. She would probably come running in at any minute.

But Brit appeared instead. She smiled as she passed Mark's table.

"Hey, Brit, you see Sharee around?" he asked.

"She's in school. I saw her this morning," Brit said. She passed, then as if on second thought said, "You know what, Mark? Sharee is a fun girl. She likes to have fun. You can't be so serious if you want the girl to stick around."

"Why?" Mark asked nervously. "Did she say something to you about me?"

Brit got a strange look on her face. "No," she said in a guarded voice, "but I was just putting two and two together, you know what I'm saying?"

Mark couldn't eat much as he sat alone pondering Sharee's absence and Brit's strange behavior. Something was going on. The only bright spot in Mark's life these days was Sharee. Once in a while he talked to a couple of guys about sports, but Sharee was his only true friend. He looked forward to seeing her every day.

Mark had a science class with Sharee at the end of the day. It was the only class they shared. He kept wondering if she would be there, and if so, what would she say?

Sharee was already at her desk when Mark walked in. He slowed alongside her desk and said, "Missed you at lunch."

"Oh, yeah, I'm sorry. I got to talking with somebody and time just got away from me," Sharee said. "I wasn't very hungry anyway."

Maybe it was just Mark's imagination, but she seemed different. She seemed to be lying. Mark always marveled that such a special girl would like him, and now he thought maybe she had come to her senses and didn't like him anymore. Maybe hanging out with a moody, skinny loner was getting old for her.

As Mark was leaving school that afternoon, he noticed Sharee talking to a tall guy who was on the Bunche Blasters basketball team. His name was Scott Jones, and girls flocked around him like pigeons at a feeder. Sharee seemed to be having an animated conversation.

Mark's hands tightened in frustration. He wasn't really angry at Sharee. He just wanted her to be up front. He didn't blame her if she was losing interest in him, but he thought she should be honest about it.

....

When Mark got home, he found his dad working on his computer again. But this time, the minute Mark walked in, he turned in his swivel chair and got up. "Hey, Mark, what's with you going to see Pops? He called me and told me you dropped in out of the blue."

Mark stuck his hands in his pockets and said, "I haven't seen him in a while, and I thought I should."

"Pops said you weren't yourself, Mark," his dad said, his dark, piercing eyes narrowing.

Not myself? Mark questioned silently. How would his grandfather know? He didn't even know Mark. "What a funny thing for him to say," Mark said aloud.

Mark's dad linked his fingers and kneaded them nervously. He always did that when he was deep in thought. "You were asking him about your mother. That's what he said. What would make you think he'd know anything about her? He had very little to do with her," his dad said.

"Sometimes I'm curious about her," Mark said.

"Your grandma and grandpa could help you there," his dad said. "She was their daughter."

Mark nodded. His grandparents had already told him many pretty stories. Like the one of her as a little girl catching lightning bugs on Lake Michigan. They had also told him about her joyful teenage years. But they had never talked about her life with his dad.

"Grandpa and Grandma are nice," Mark blurted out. He had liked living with them. Maybe if Mark had continued living with his grandparents, the terrible memories of that night would have faded by now.

Mark's dad continued to stare suspiciously at Mark. He seemed to realize in some vague way that his son was deeply troubled. "You weren't too anxious to come live with me after you'd lived with your grandparents," he said.

"Yeah," Mark said.

"Would you rather be with them now?" Mark's dad asked.

Mark was becoming nervous. His father's eyes looked intense. Usually he showed little emotion, but now he kneaded his fingers and a nerve jumped visibly in his temple. That made Mark uncomfortable. Maybe his dad had begun to guess the source of Mark's moodiness. Maybe he was growing afraid that Mark had heard something that night or even *seen* something. Even though Mark never talked about that night, maybe his dad suspected he had buried dreadful memories.

"No," Mark lied. "I mean, it's okay living here. My grandparents are great and everything. I like to hang out there sometimes. But it's . . . uh . . . okay here . . . "

"I've always noticed that you are very distant with me, Mark. But lately it's been getting worse. I try to tell myself that it's because of your age, that all guys your age sort of drift away from their parents. But when I talked with Pops, well, he said the same thing I've been feeling. He said you didn't strike him as okay, Mark," his dad said.

Mark shrugged. "Some stuff at school . . . " he muttered softly. "Girlfriend stuff."

His dad seemed to relax a little and even crack a smile. "I hear you," he said in a rueful voice.

Mark escaped eagerly to his room and closed the door behind him. Mark remembered when he was in fourth grade, five years after his mother's death. The teacher had noted that he was "withdrawn." She had seen on Mark's file that his mother was deceased, and she had attributed Mark's lonely personality to that fact.

The teacher had called Mark's father in for a conference with a special counselor. Mark recalled sitting with his father in the counseling room as the woman talked about his mom's death. He couldn't remember much of the conference, although he did remember his dad turning to him and asking, "You don't need to talk to anybody about your feelings, do you?" Mark could tell that his father wanted him to say no. So that was what he had said. Later, when the counselor questioned him alone, he said the same thing.

On the way home from the counseling session, his dad had turned to his nine-year-old son and said, "Wasn't that silly, Mark? Why, you were sound asleep the night your mother had that accident. That lady kept talking about trauma and shock. But you didn't even know what was going on that night, right?"

"Yeah," Mark had said, lying.

Now Mark wondered if his dad continued to worry that Mark had maybe seen or heard something. Just as the terror of the night haunted Mark, maybe it haunted his father, who had to wonder each day if Mark had seen the "accident." Perhaps his dad wondered if his small son had left his bed that night to investigate the terrifying sounds. His dad couldn't know for sure that Mark was hiding under his covers the whole time. He didn't know that, and maybe he was frightened that his son was a witness to murder . . .

Mark sat on the edge of his bed perspiring. He needed to find out what happened that night. He rummaged desperately through his mind until he came up with the city newspaper. They probably had an item in the newspaper after his mom died. There must be copies of old newspapers down in the newspaper room of the library. The newer newspapers were on the computer, but he expected the older papers were on microfilm. Maybe there would be something there, something to put his mind at rest.

....

After school the next day, Mark went down to the central library. The librarian took him to the newspaper room and sat him down before the microfilm machine.

Mark grasped how the machine worked quickly, and soon he was rolling back 12 years to newspapers dated right after his mom's death. When he saw the headline "Woman dies in fall," Mark gasped. Mark took a deep breath and started reading:

"Belle Lee Ryder, 23, Glenn Falls, was fatally injured after falling down the stairs at her home on Friday night. She had been home alone with her four-year-old son, who was sleeping upstairs when the accident occurred. The victim's husband, Harry Ryder, returned home from work to find her unconscious on the floor. She was pronounced dead at Tri-County Hospital."

That wasn't what had happened at all. She hadn't been home alone. Someone else had been there.

Mark made a copy of the article and stumbled from the library on shaky legs.

5 AT SCHOOL THE next day, Mark walked into his English class. He noticed some snickering behind him, and he glanced back to see Brit whispering to another girl. The moment he looked at them, they stopped laughing and opened their textbooks. Mark was sure they were giggling about him.

Joey Lipovich, a tall, lanky boy who sat in the back row in English class, talked to Mark sometimes. They both had tried out for the track team but had been refused for lack of athletic skill. Once in a while they got together for pizza and to shoot pool. Joey wasn't exactly Mark's friend, but he was close. So after school that day, Mark caught up to Joey as they were both leaving the campus.

"Want to get some pizza?" Mark asked Joey. "They've got a deal today. Double cheese, double pepperoni, same price."

"You're on," Joey said.

When the boys were in the pizza place

eating, Mark said, "Joey, a couple of times today in classes, I caught kids behind me snickering. I think *I* was the joke. Do you know what's going on?"

"Yeah," Joey said. "It's about Scott and Sharee and how she's hanging with him now. He just snapped his fingers, and she came running."

"And what are they snickering about? That I'm out in the cold, and I haven't got a clue? Is that it?" Mark demanded.

Joey shrugged. "Sharee is going around telling all her friends how bad she feels about dumping you and stuff, but she doesn't know what to do. The big joke is when she's going to drop the bomb on you, I guess," he said.

"How did Sharee and Scott get together so fast?" Mark asked. "We went to the splash park last Saturday. I thought we had a good time."

"Scott Jones likes a turn at every pretty girl. Sharee has always been interested in Scott, but she never thought that he might be interested in her. Then all of a sudden he comes on to her and she freaks," Joey said. "You know how girls are. They're looking for the best dude around, and we're not it."

Mark tried to be casual about it even though it hurt. "Sharee and I didn't have anything special going. We just hung out together for lunch. She can go with anybody she wants. I don't care," he said.

"Yeah, but Sharee told Brit you were like real shaky and kind of a sad case, and she didn't want to push you over the edge. That's what Brit said anyway. I don't know if Sharee really told her that or if it's Brit making stuff up again," Joey said.

"That really bothers me," Mark snapped. "When they're talking about me like that, it really fries me."

Mark felt bitterness wash over him, like a hot wind searing frail spring grass. It was just as he had thought all along— Sharee Parks never liked him. He was just an interesting diversion. He was a project for her. She enjoyed working on him like a scientist likes to manipulate a lab rat. Make a special maze and see how the poor, confused creature acts. It's not like the scientist cares about the poor rat. It's just interesting to see what it does under different experiments.

Mark left most of his pizza on his plate. He took a swallow of soda and headed back to school. Sharee would still be there. She was in the Bunche High glee club, and they were practicing for a tribute to Dr. Martin Luther King. Mark figured that if he waited outside the auditorium he could talk to her.

As Mark stood waiting, listening to the glee club singing, he could pick out Sharee's sweet soprano. She had a solo. Mark's hands formed into fists so tight that his fingers ached. He hated Sharee. There was no doubt of that. He hated her with every fiber of his being.

Is this how Mark's dad felt that night toward his mom? Mark wondered. Had she done something to make him feel small, despised, humiliated? Moe had hinted that his mom was no angel. Maybe she enjoyed taunting his dad with the attention of other guys. Maybe she was just playing, enjoying the flirting, and his dad lost it. Maybe that's what happened on that terrible night.

Mark did not want to be like his father

in any way. He didn't want to feel the rage he was now feeling, but he could not make it go away.

It was not so much that Sharee was going with another guy. It was that she was making Mark the laughingstock of the school, letting everybody know how much he would be hurting.

Finally the glee club practice ended, and the students came filing out into the crisp night air.

"Mark!" Sharee gasped when she saw him. She looked almost frightened.

"Sharee, could we go somewhere private?" Mark said. "I just need to tell you something."

Sharee hesitated. She exchanged a nervous look with the girl beside her. It was obvious that Sharee had already told everybody about the strange, lonely boy she had befriended. Everyone probably believed he was some weird psycho. Mark's hatred surged in his chest, causing his heart to pound.

"I just need a couple of minutes," he said tersely.

"Sure, okay," Sharee said, walking

slowly toward him. They moved to a deserted walkway alongside the auditorium, out of earshot of anybody else.

"Sharee, I don't care if you have a new boyfriend," Mark began.

"Mark!" Sharee said, looking stricken. "It's not . . . "

"Let me talk," Marked snapped, cutting her off. "I don't care if you and Scott are hanging out. I couldn't care less, okay? What I hate is that you've got everybody believing I'm some weirdo who can't take being dumped."

"Mark, I didn't . . . " Sharee said.

"How do you think it makes me feel when everybody is snickering behind my back, Sharee? Look at poor stupid Mark Ryder. His girlfriend dumped him for another guy, and she's afraid to tell him because he's crazy," Mark said bitterly.

"Mark, that's not true," Sharee said desperately. "I never . . . "

"Just do me one favor, Sharee," Mark said. "Stop talking about me. Just leave me alone. When you and your snotty little girlfriends are getting together, leave me out of the party. Pretend I'm dead, okay? I don't need you. I don't need anybody, and I especially don't need a two-faced girl like you."

Tears began rolling down Sharee's face. "Oh, M—Mark," she wept, "I really do care about you. I never meant to hurt you."

"You never cared any more for me than a scientist cares for the white rats he's poisoning. That's what I was to you, Sharee. A lab rat. If you ever cared about me, you would have treated me with a little respect, you know? You would have done a good thing and told me you wanted to date another guy," Mark said.

Sharee began sobbing.

"Just stay out of my life. Stop talking about me," Mark said.

"I wasn't talking about you," Sharee protested.

"Drop dead," Mark hissed at her before turning sharply and walking away in the darkness.

He was numb with anger. He put every ounce of malice he had into the "drop dead" comment. Mark was drenched in his own perspiration. With sickening, shocking clarity, he felt like he had climbed into his father's skin and experienced what his dad may have felt the night Mark's mom had died. Mark fell into a run, heading for home, trying to outdistance his own pain.

....

On the following Sunday, Mark made his usual trip to his grandparents' for dinner. He loved his Sunday routine. He always arrived early for dinner and helped his grandpa with chores while his grandma prepared the meal. It was the only place he felt truly comfortable. The years he had spent at his grandparents' place were happy ones, despite the memory that haunted him.

"I've made chicken paprika, your favorite, sweetie-pie," his grandma said, beaming at Mark.

"Thanks, Grandma," Mark said, giving her a hug.

After dinner, the three of them went into the living room for coffee and dessert—his grandma's famous apple strudel. After some routine conversation,

Mark said, "My dad asked me if I'd rather live here with you guys . . . "

Mark's grandparents weren't very old— they were only in their sixties. And they looked much younger than that. Mark knew a lot of guys his age wanted no part of their grandparents, but Mark didn't feel like that.

"So what did you tell your dad?" his grandma asked.

"I told him I wanted to stay where I was," Mark said.

"Good for you," his grandpa said. "It would have hurt your dad if you'd said anything else."

"But it was a lie," Mark blurted. "I'd rather live here. I'd like to move in here tomorrow."

His grandma and grandpa looked at each other, puzzled.

"Mark, you don't know what you're saying," Mark's grandpa said.

"Yeah, I do," Mark said, emboldened to say more since he had opened the subject up. "I feel weird living with Dad. He's a spooky guy. I don't feel like I even know him."

"Your dad is a quiet man," Mark's grandpa said. "He's not easy to get to know. But he's smart; he's hardworking."

Mark felt such strong emotion welling up inside him. It was so strong that he couldn't eat any of the dessert. He gulped down some coffee and said, "I'm afraid of my father."

Mark was shocked by what he had said. It never would have happened if the pressure hadn't built up so much. Mark felt both his grandparents staring at him.

"Has your father ever laid a violent hand on you?" his grandpa asked sternly.

"No, he hasn't," Mark admitted.

"Why are you afraid of him then, boy?" his grandpa demanded. "What is this all about?"

"Oh, dear," his grandma moaned, "a boy should not be afraid of his own daddy!"

Marks' heart was pounding. He felt like tanks were rolling over his chest. He closed his eyes. *He had to tell somebody.* For 12 years he had kept it all bottled up inside. Mark felt as if he might explode unless he let it out. He knew it would never go away.

6 "I . . . I REMEMBER STUFF about the night Mom died that I've never talked about," Mark said, barely above a whisper, unsure if, at any moment, he would take it all back and tell his grandparents he was lying.

Mark's grandpa leaned forward, a startled look on his face. "You were barely four years old! A baby!" he gasped.

"I woke up and they were . . . yelling and screaming. My mom and dad were fighting. I had never heard them like that before. I was so scared," Mark said.

His grandma drew closer, a look of horror on her face. "Are you sure it wasn't just a nightmare, child? Are you sure you're not remembering a childhood nightmare?" she asked.

"I'm sure I heard the fighting and the screaming, and then somebody . . . I guess it was . . . uh . . . you know . . . Mom falling," Mark stammered.

"Mark," his grandpa said, "your father

was at work. He worked late at the lab. He had just come home, when he saw your mother lying there at the bottom of the stairs, scarcely alive. He called 911."

Mark shook his head. "I heard them fighting. I swear I heard them fighting, and I was so scared I tried to crawl deep under the covers. But I couldn't shut it out," he said.

"He never said anything about an argument," Mark's grandpa said. An anger had come into the older man's eyes, almost a rage. A righteous fury.

"I *know* it happened. All my life I have been wishing it hadn't happened. I kept hoping the memory would go away, but it hasn't. It haunts me. Every time I look at my father, I wonder about that night," Mark said.

"Mark," his grandma began, "your parents were married for five years. I was close to my daughter, your mother. She had her ups and downs with your daddy, but she never once said he yelled at her, or heaven forbid, hurt her in any way. She would have told me."

Mark buried his face in his hands. "I

had never heard them fighting like that before. Sometimes they'd mumble at each other, and I'd know they were arguing about something. But then it'd be over real quick. This was different," he said.

"And because of that memory you're afraid of your father?" his grandpa asked.

"Yeah, that mostly. And then he seems to be brooding all the time, like he's haunted too. I look at him and I sort of think I know what's on his mind. He's thinking about Mom and what happened . . . that night . . . " Mark said.

The atmosphere in the living room had become heavy and grim. Mark was already regretting opening his mouth because now things would never be the same again. But he had to share this with somebody, and so he did. It was either that or lose his mind.

"Mark, have you ever mentioned any of this to your father?" his grandpa asked.

"No," Mark cried, shocked that his grandpa would even imagine such a thing.

Before Mark left to go home that evening, his grandma hugged him for a long time. "Don't you worry, baby," she whispered. "Things aren't as bad as you think. It will be all right, child. It really will be all right."

His grandpa stood there, his face set with resolution. "Do you have any friends you could spend the night with?" he asked.

"No, I'll be okay staying with my dad," Mark said.

"Well, we'll be talking to your father, Mark," his grandpa replied. "Maybe it would be best if you weren't there."

"No," Mark said. "I'd like to be there."

Mark didn't go right home from his grandparents' house. He called Joey to see if he wanted to shoot some pool and just hang out.

The boys ended up in a pool hall a couple of blocks from Mark's home. They played a few games then got some sodas and drove to Joey's house. As they sat at Joey's house, Mark explained everything—about his mom, the fear concerning his dad, and the latest development with his grandparents.

"What was your mom like?" Joey finally asked.

"She was wonderful. And so pretty. Here, look at this picture of her," Mark pulled the yearbook from his backpack and opened to a picture of his mom. "Brit gave this yearbook to me."

Joey's expression turned to confusion, so Mark continued explaining. "See, Brit's mom and my mom were in the same graduating class, so Brit gave me their high school yearbook. She said I could borrow it for as long as I wanted. I've had it a while but haven't looked at it closely yet."

"Oh, I get it," Joey said.

The two boys flipped through the book. Photos of his mother doing sports and clowning around like teenagers do filled the book. It gave Mark a funny feeling to think his mom looked just like the girls he went to school with, a big, silly grin on her face as she smiled for the camera. And to think, only six years after that, she was dead.

Mark's mother was a good tennis player and a softball star. She was on the swimming team too.

Mark scanned the photos and took

particular interest in the ones of her on the homecoming court. She looked amazing in her teal gown and heels. He also took interest in the man who stood next to her in all of the photos. Mark assumed he was the homecoming king, judging by the crown on his head. The guy was tall, muscular, and well-built.

"I wonder who he is," Mark said aloud.

"Hmm," Joey said. "Look at the caption." Mark's eyes scanned down to the caption underneath the photo. It read, "Reggie Fitch and Belle Lee Crosley."

"Your dad isn't a bad-looking dude, but he's no Reggie Fitch," Joey said. "I wonder why your mom dumped Reggie for your dad."

Mark fell silent. His dad was pretty short, and Reggie was well over six feet tall. It appeared that Reggie had a lot of charm. You could see that. In one picture he was grinning from ear to ear, and Mark's mom was perched on his shoulders. Mark's dad would never have done anything that silly.

Mark couldn't figure it out either. Why didn't his mom marry the handsome, charming Reggie Fitch?

If she had, maybe she'd be alive now.

Almost surely she'd be alive now . . . .

The boys went over to Bunche High and played some one-on-one basketball on the hoops there. Then they crossed the street to a mini-mart for snacks.

"Man," Joey said, "next year we're going to be seniors, and I haven't got a clue what I'm going to do."

"I want to keep going in math and science," Mark said. "I want to be an astronomer. I'd like to live in some observatory in the Arizona desert and just watch the stars. Then I wouldn't have to bother with people at all."

Mark's cell phone rang.

"Where are you?" Mark's grandpa asked.

"I'm with Joey," Mark said.

"I called your father. We talked," Mr. Crosley said. "He sounded very strange. I told him it wasn't a good idea for you to be there in that apartment as long as things were like they are. He wants to talk to you, Mark, so he's coming over here. Can you be at our house pretty quick?"

Mark felt numb all over. "Okay," he said.

As Joey drove Mark over to his grandparents' house, Mark's mind was spinning wildly. He felt like his brains were caught in the dryer at the laundromat.

Mark dreaded facing his father. It made him sick to his stomach to look into the man's eyes and talk about this thing. He wished he could just get out of Joey's truck and run to the bus stop.

But he had to face it. He had taken the coward's way long enough. It was time to be a man.

When Joey dropped Mark off, Mark saw his dad's car parked in his grandparents' driveway. As Mark walked up the driveway, his father stepped from the car.

"I need to talk to you," Mark's father said grimly. "I think it would be better if we talked in the car, if you don't mind."

"Sure, okay," Mark said. He got in the front seat.

Mark took a quick glance at his father. The man's eyes seemed afire. Mark had never seen such a look on his father's face before. He looked like death itself.

"Your grandfather called me. He told me you shared something with him that you have never shared with anybody else," his dad said slowly. "Naturally, Mark, it all came as a terrible shock to me."

Mark felt an icy wind blow across his soul. He should have known all this would happen when he talked to his grandparents. He probably did know. He had to have known his world for the past 12 years would come to an end.

"So," his dad said in a measured voice, "you woke up the night your mother died? You believe you heard your mother and me having some kind of an argument."

Mark glanced at his grandparents' front window. He saw the curtain move. They were watching closely. They would move fast if anything went wrong, if Mark was in any danger. They would call 911, but even before that his grandpa would come charging out with the weapon he had a license for.

"I . . . uh . . . did wake up. I heard you and Mom . . . uh . . . yelling and stuff and then I heard her fall," Mark said.

"It's not possible, Mark. You must be remembering a very vivid nightmare," his dad said emphatically.

"No. I'm sure it happened," Mark said.

His dad's voice turned cold. "After all these years, you suddenly have a clear memory of something that happened 12 years ago? You were a small child—only a four-year-old. I am amazed and angry that you would enlarge this nightmare into something real. You have upset your grandparents and turned all our lives upside down," he said.

When Mark looked at his father, the man's features seemed to blur.

7 "I'M SORRY," Mark said brokenly, "but I heard you guys fighting."

"*What fight*? What are you talking about?" his dad demanded. "Your grandparents told me what you told them, but it did not happen. I was working in the lab until very late that night. It was almost 11:00 when I got home. When I opened the door, I saw your mother lying on the floor at the foot of the stairs. It was the most horrible moment of my life. I didn't know that she was fatally injured, but I could see by the position of her head that she was horribly injured. I could see that her neck was bent grotesquely by the fall." Mark's dad was breathing heavily now, shaking with more emotion than Mark had ever seen in him before. A light sheen of perspiration had broken out on his face.

"But I heard you guys yelling and screaming for a long time before I heard the thump, thump of her falling," Mark insisted.

"You were a baby!" his dad yelled. "How could you be sure of anything? You were just four years old. You were just having a bad dream. You probably watched some stupid, violent cartoon. Your mother was always letting you watch those awful shows. Then you fell asleep with these violent sounds and images in your head, and when you woke up, you imagined you heard fighting. Can't you see that's what happened, Mark?"

His dad was leaning forward in the seat beside Mark, as if by the force of his body language he would drive home the truth. Mark felt himself growing more intimidated, the more emotional his dad got. "Well . . . uh . . . it seemed real," Mark stammered.

"Of course it seemed real. When you're four years old you don't know reality from fantasy. Half the time you can't tell the difference between make-believe and what's actually happening." Some of the tension was easing from his dad's voice.

"I guess," Mark said. He reached for the door handle. He wanted to get out of the car. He wanted to be anywhere but here.

"Wait," his dad said, "we're not finished talking. I want you to tell me exactly what you think you heard that night."

"You and Mom screaming at each other. Mom yelled a lot, but you never did. So that scared me more than anything—to hear you sounding so weird. You sounded so mad that you didn't even sound like my dad anymore. You'd turned into a . . . a monster or something. A whole different person. I was so scared . . . " Mark said.

Mark's father stared at him as he continued the story. "I tried to crawl deeper under the covers. I wanted the sound to go away. But it wouldn't. It just kept going. And then, you know, I heard this thumping sound. Like something heavy hitting the stairs. It was like thud, thud, thud. And then it stopped. I didn't know what it was, but I was so scared."

The nerve in his dad's temple twitched, and his eyes widened. He looked horrified.

"And then suddenly, it was quiet," Mark recalled. "I don't know how long. Not long, though. Then the sirens came, and strangers were coming in the house. I found out later that Mom had fallen down the stairs and died . . . So I figured that was what made the thud, thud sounds . . . you know, her falling. And all of it keeps coming back to me, and I can't forget it." Mark buried his face in his hands and cried.

His dad didn't speak for a moment, then he said, "Maybe your mother had the TV on. Maybe somebody was yelling on the TV."

"I could tell it was Mom's voice. You sounded weird, but Mom sounded like she always did when she was mad. It was how she yelled at me when I tried to cross the street without looking both ways," Mark said.

"But it did not happen," his dad said. "Mark, do you realize what you're saying with all this nonsense? You're saying your mother and I were having a violent argument just before she fell, and if that's true, then it's my fault your mother died. It's like you're accusing me of killing her!"

"I'm not saying that," Mark protested. But he *was* saying that. He had been thinking that for a long time. Every time he looked at his silent, brooding father, he thought that. Did he hurt his mom? Did he scare her into falling? Had he pushed her out of anger and started her fatal plunge down the stairs?

"You better stay with your grandparents tonight," his dad said. "Think about all this, Mark, and we'll talk tomorrow."

Mark got very little sleep that night. He thought he would feel better if the secret was out in the open, but he only felt worse.

....

Mark went to school the next day as usual, going through his classes like a zombie. He didn't even write down the assignments. Then, after school, as he was leaving the campus, he saw his father pull up.

Mark had never seen his father looking so distraught. He looked like he hadn't slept much. There were deep circles under his eyes. He was usually very well-groomed, but now his shirt was rumpled and his hair uncombed.

Mark rode home with his dad, and they

walked in the apartment in heavy silence. Mark sat opposite his father in the living room.

"I talked to your mother's parents today," his dad began. "They've been mulling everything over since you told them that stuff. We talked for a long time. I . . . don't think they believe me anymore . . . "

Mark said nothing. He clasped his hands on his lap to keep them from trembling.

"Your grandparents told me they have a lot of questions. I couldn't answer them to their satisfaction," his dad continued in a grim monotone.

Mark was swept with a feeling of overwhelming guilt.

What have I done? Mark asked himself. I've destroyed my family. I've destroyed the relationship between my dad and my grandparents. I've put my father under terrible suspicion . . .

"I'm sorry, Dad," Mark mumbled.

His dad smiled in a terrible way. "It's rather late for that, isn't it, Mark? Tell me, why have you done this, anyway? Is your life here so miserable that you went to such extreme ends to get away? Do you hate me so much that you found it necessary to create a fantasy to destroy me?" he asked.

"I didn't create a fantasy," Mark stammered. His father was looking at him with anger, or maybe more than anger. Maybe hatred.

"You never heard anything that night because it did not happen. I never realized you were such a sick, vicious boy, Mark. I had no idea," his dad said bitterly.

"Dad, don't talk like that," Mark cried. "This thing has been driving me crazy all these years. I just couldn't keep it bottled up anymore. I didn't want to hurt anybody! I swear, I didn't want to hurt anybody!"

"Don't give me that," his dad snapped. "You're 16 years old. You're not a child. You knew darn well what would happen if you told your grandparents that I was violently fighting with their daughter before she fell. Belle Lee was their only child. The sun rose and fell on her for them. Now they're wondering if I killed her. You've stuck a knife in my back, Mark."

Guilt, fear, and regret washed over Mark in great tidal waves. He was sick to his stomach. He wished he were dead. He wished he had never been born. He thought he would vomit at any moment, or maybe pass out.

His dad stood up, and for a moment, Mark thought his dad was going to attack him. He looked that mad, that distraught.

But, instead, his dad stopped a few feet from Mark. "I don't want you here with me after what has happened. I told your grandparents that I'd rather you stay with them for now. They said it was all right. So pack some things and go. On the weekend you can move the rest of your stuff," he said.

Mark was stunned. It was all happening so fast. He didn't know what he thought would happen after he blurted out the truth to his grandparents. Maybe he just hadn't thought it through at all.

Or maybe, unconsciously, he did know what he was doing. Maybe he hoped just what was happening would happen. He had never wanted to live with his father. And now he wouldn't anymore.

"Your grandfather will be here in a few minutes, so pack a suitcase. You can get a friend to help you load up your stuff on Saturday." His dad's voice was flat and unemotional. "I'll pay for your room and board at your grandparents."

"Dad, listen, *I'm sorry*," Mark said.

Mark's dad gave Mark a withering look and walked away. He went into his bedroom and closed the door behind him.

On Saturday morning, Mark returned to his dad's apartment. With Joey's help, Mark moved his computer, TV, and clothes.

When Joey's truck was loaded up, Mark hesitated before getting in. His father stood in the doorway, and Mark looked warily at him. "Uh . . . Dad, you going to call or anything when I'm over there?" Mark asked.

"I'll keep in touch," his dad said tersely. His hands were stuck in his pockets. He looked like he was about to weep or go mad, one or the other.

"Dad . . . I," Mark began, not knowing what to say. He was sorry this was happening. But it wasn't his fault that he remembered that terrible night and couldn't hold it inside anymore. Mark was sorry everything had turned upside down like this and his family was shattered.

His dad turned away and walked back into the apartment.

Mark climbed in the pickup with Joey.

"This has got to be a bad day for you," Joey said.

"Yeah," Mark said. Mark looked back at the apartment where he had lived for the past eight years. He wondered if his father was inside watching out the window, watching Mark disappear around the corner. Mark didn't see his father watching, but he was probably there, behind the curtains.

"Your grandparents seem nice," Joey said.

"Yeah, they're great," Mark said. He felt so empty inside. A great ache throbbed inside him, taking his breath.

Mark thought to himself that he really

didn't want to be with his father anymore, so this was a good thing. But he still loved his father. He was afraid of him, but he still loved him. Mark ached with sorrow at the pain he knew he was causing his father.

Mark could not remember ever feeling as totally desolate as he now felt. He had lost his mother 12 years ago. For the past 12 years he had been, little by little, losing his father too. As each year went by, the suspicions deepened.

Today, Mark feared, he had truly lost his father for good. And that fueled a grief he could hardly bear.

8 ON SUNDAY MORNING it felt strange waking up in his grandparents' house. At home with his father, they didn't make much of breakfast. His dad would grab a nutrition bar and a cup of black coffee, and Mark would dig into a package of doughnuts. Now, as Mark opened his eyes, he smelled bacon frying. There were voices coming from the kitchen.

It was just how it used to be when Mark was young and lived there. His grandma was an early riser, and she made huge breakfasts. "Breakfast is the most important meal in the day," his grandma would say. "It's the foundation for the rest of the day."

Mark got dressed and joined his grandparents at the kitchen table. There were eggs, waffles, and bacon already out.

Nobody wanted to talk about what had happened and why Mark was there. Everybody was thinking about it, but nobody wanted to talk about it. Not now. Not on a sunny Sunday morning.

"We go to church at 11:00, honey," his grandma said. "You don't have to go if you don't want to, but we'd sure like for you to come. I still sing in the choir."

Mark's grandparents had always been so nice to him. He loved them very much. When Mark lived with his father he didn't go to church, and he didn't feel like going now. But he thought he should for his grandmother's sake. She was so proud of singing in the choir, raising her loud soprano voice in the Many Voices of Praise Choir. "Sure, I'll go," he said, bringing a pleased smile to his grandma's face.

The three of them went to the small church where Mark's mom had been buried. Mark vaguely remembered her lying in the white casket surrounded by so many flowers. People were crying and loudly moaning. The minister shouted out a rousing sermon that Mark did not understand. All Mark clearly remembered was that everybody was crying and hugging one another, and his mommy was gone.

Now, today, the Many Voices of Praise Choir donned their bright blue choir robes. They sang joyful songs and swayed back and forth and called out "hallelujahs" while they clapped their hands.

After church, Mark and his grandparents finally talked about what they had been avoiding all morning.

"I suppose your father told you it got pretty heated around here the other day," his grandpa began.

"Sort of," Mark admitted.

"Well, Mark, we never doubted your father's account of what happened that night," his grandpa said. "But now we know differently. We could hardly believe that he would lie about it, but it looks like he did."

Mark's grandma looked sad, but his grandpa was more angry than sad. "It's pretty obvious why the man lied. It's a hard thing to face, boy, for all of us. I guess we were all so anxious to believe it was just an accident that we never really stopped to wonder," he said.

"We always tried so hard to like your daddy," Mark's grandma continued. "But he was never like us."

"He's always been a strange one," Mark's grandpa said, "so quiet. Keeping to himself. Not interested in sports, just his work . . ."

"Reggie was just the opposite," his grandma said suddenly. "That boy was so full of life. Always laughing and yelling. Why you could hear him halfway around town! He was nice and tall. I'd never seen such a handsome boy."

"We thought your mom would marry Reggie Fitch," his grandpa said regretfully. "Everybody thought so. All Belle Lee's friends. Everybody. But then, all of a sudden, she meets this strange little man with the frown on his face—why he was barely as tall as Belle Lee."

"We're not saying your father wasn't a nice-looking fellow," his grandma said hastily. "He was so intelligent and different though . . . we couldn't understand why Belle Lee went for him."

"Sounds like this Reggie Fitch was like Scott Jones," Mark said. "Scott's a guy at school, good-looking, athletic. All the girls are crazy about him."

"Yes, Reggie *was* popular. His father sold antique cars and hot rods, and everybody would hang out over there," his grandpa said. "But he loved Belle Lee. She was the girl he wanted to be with. You could see that."

"They were so precious together," his grandma said wistfully. She shook her head. Mark knew exactly where her mind was going. If Belle Lee Crosley had stuck with Reggie Fitch, then they'd been married. Things would all be different now. The Crosleys' only daughter would still be alive.

....

When Mark arrived at school on Monday morning, he noticed Sharee standing on the walk he used to get to his first class. She seemed to be waiting for him. Mark didn't want to see her. He turned and took another route toward class. But Sharee saw the evasive action and rushed after him.

"Mark, I've got to talk to you," she said.

"I'm late for history class. Mr. Smith has a fit when we're late. I'm in enough trouble already in that class. I haven't read the assignments for three days," Mark said, looking past the girl.

"Please, Mark, meet me for lunch. Please!" Sharee called after him. "In the cafeteria, in our corner."

Mark walked faster. He pretended he didn't hear her. He was in no mood to listen to any more of her weepy apologies that would justify dumping him. He was really hurt when she went to another guy so fast, but he could have forgiven her for that. It was the fact that she thought of him as some pathetic loser that he couldn't take.

Maybe Scott had dumped her, and she wondered if the welcome mat for her was still out at desperate Mark Ryder's door.

Well, it isn't, Mark thought coldly.

Mark barely listened during history and math class. As he went to the cafeteria he looked around for Joey, hoping he could join him for lunch. Then he remembered Joey left school early to get his braces fixed. It would be another lonely lunchtime, but now even worse because of the situation at home.

Mark got his meatloaf and lumpy mashed potatoes and sat down forlornly.

Sharee appeared. "I know you hate me, but at least you can listen to what I have to say. Then I'll go eat somewhere else," she said, holding her tray.

"I don't hate you," Mark said as he stared at his meatloaf. "I just don't need to hear a lot of trash."

Sharee sat down and put her tray on the table. "I'm ashamed of myself because when Scott asked me out, I went for it. Not because I like Scott or anything, but it's *such* a big deal when he asks you out. I just forgot everything. I know it was rude and creepy of me to talk to my friends about us, but it wasn't like you think. I was just feeling guilty and I had to talk about it. I didn't speak badly about you, Mark, I swear I didn't. Mark, haven't you ever made a mistake?"

"Yeah," Mark said, stabbing the hard, dry meatloaf with his fork. He drowned it in ketchup before he tried to eat it.

"Well, I made a big mistake. Scott is a pompous jerk, and being with him wasn't fun at all. He kept talking about himself the whole time. He wasn't the least bit interested in anything I had to say. I just freaked when Scott Jones, this awesome jock, showed an interest in me. But then I realized I didn't want to be with him at all. I wanted to be with you," Sharee said.

"So now you want to crawl back to old loner Mark," Mark said angrily.

"Mark, I never pitied you. You were all wrong when you said that. I've always respected you, and I really liked being with you because you're real. You're not fake like Scott," Sharee said. "Well, thanks for letting me say my piece. I won't bother you anymore, Mark. I just wanted you to know the truth." Sharee got up and started to leave.

Mark couldn't believe it when he heard his own voice say, "No, wait."

In spite of himself and his pride, Mark was willing to take Sharee back. Especially now that his life was so awful. He needed her desperately.

Sharee quickly sat down and looked at Mark's meatloaf. "It tastes much better with salsa on it. I always keep a couple packets of salsa for the food around here.

When meatloaf is that bad, only salsa makes it edible. Here have one."

Mark accepted the offer, and the meatloaf improved dramatically. Mark gave Sharee a sheepish grin. Then he said, "I'm not living with my dad anymore. I'm living with my grandparents."

"How come?" Sharee asked.

"My dad thought it'd be better," Mark said. He couldn't share his terrible personal story with her.

"I'd hate living with *my* grandparents," Sharee said. "They are so strict!"

"Mine are nice," Mark said.

"Your mom's parents, huh?" Sharee asked gently.

"Yeah," Mark said.

Sharee looked sad. "I read somewhere that when a person loses a parent and they're under five years old, it sort of marks them. You don't trust life as much anymore. I guess that's why you're kind of sad, Mark. I know that my mom and I fight a lot, but I can't imagine not having her in my life. I mean, I don't want her to *ever* die," Sharee said.

Mark nodded.

The two finished lunch quietly. They exchanged no words, only glances and smiles.

....

Mark's walk home to his grandparents' house was not much farther than when he lived at his dad's apartment. It was just in a different direction.

Sometimes Mark's father would pick him up at Bunche High and drive him home. They'd usually stop at a convenience store for a hot dog and soda. His dad hated to prepare food. He'd much rather buy something already made. Now, as Mark left the campus, he was shocked to see his father's car across the street.

His dad turned and looked right at Mark, but he made no attempt to pick him up. He just sped away.

Mark felt a rush of mixed emotion— sadness, regret, maybe even fear.

9 MARK SAW BRIT'S mother picking her up at the curb, and on impulse Mark walked over. Mark knew his mom and Mrs. Walsh had been best friends. The yearbook was full of them, heads together, laughing, clowning around. Now Mark wondered if his mom had ever confided in her best friend about the troubles she was having in her marriage.

"Hi, Mrs. Walsh. Listen, would you ever have time to talk to me? I, uh . . . wanted to ask you about my mother's school days . . . I guess you guys were tight, huh?" Mark asked.

Mrs. Walsh immediately looked sympathetic. Brit had probably already told her mother about poor, lonely Mark Ryder. "Sure, Mark. How about today? I'm dropping Brit off at the dance studio, then you and I could get a cinnamon bun and coffee."

"Okay," Mark said. He climbed in the

van, and after Brit had been dropped off
at the studio, they stopped at a little
coffee shop and took a booth in the
corner.

"Your mom and I were like sisters,"
Mrs. Walsh said. "Your mom was more fun
than a barrel of monkeys. Everybody liked
her."

"You were still friends when she . . . uh,
died?" Mark asked.

"Oh, we never stopped being friends.
Even after we both got married. We'd go
shopping every Tuesday, come rain or
shine. Girls' day out was a ritual not to be
tampered with. We'd even hang at the mall
after Belle had you and I had Brit. We'd
push you little guys in your strollers, and
we'd have a ball. It was hectic, managing
two little kids, but we'd handle it. Belle,
especially. She could laugh her way out of
anything," Mrs. Walsh said.

"You know what happened then," Mark
said.

Sadness crept into the woman's face.
"Of course. It was the most traumatic
thing to happen in our lives, all us girls
from that Lincoln High class. We were all

close. We'd go places together when we were juniors and seniors. I must have a million snapshots of our fun times. Belle was always in the middle of everything. When she died like that, it just shook us all to our foundations. I think going to her funeral was the saddest thing I've ever had to do. She still looked like a teenager. Like a little teen angel asleep in the white satin box . . . " Mrs. Walsh wiped away tears.

"Uh . . . I looked in the yearbook my mom is in, and she dated some guy named Reggie. Did she ever say why she dropped him for my dad?" Mark asked.

Mrs. Walsh smiled again. "Love. Belle Lee fell in love with this real quiet little man the year she started college. We were all dumbfounded. But then said she was so in love with Harry Ryder that nothing else mattered. Who can figure? I think sometimes falling in love is like getting the flu. When it hits you, you're helpless!" she said.

"You've met my dad, huh?" Mark asked.

"Several times. We'd have barbecues at each other's houses. He was always very reserved. I was surprised that Belle loved him. She was a bubble machine," Mrs. Walsh said.

"I don't remember much about my mom," Mark said. "I . . . wish I remembered more. I know she used to play with me under the jacaranda tree. And she'd always sing and laugh and stuff. I liked being with her."

"Everybody loved being with her. She was that kind of a person. Just so warm and loving," Mrs. Walsh said.

"Uh . . . she and my dad were happy, I guess," Mark blurted. "I mean, they must have been happy because . . . "

Mrs. Walsh did not answer right away. Then she smiled and said, "Of course they were happy. Your father loved Belle so much. When I went to the funeral, I was afraid the poor man would go mad right before our eyes. I have never seen such a grief-stricken husband. He never remarried, did he, Mark? I guess he couldn't replace Belle, poor man."

"And my mom loved my dad a lot too, huh?" Mark pressed. "I mean, she must have told you stuff like that. I guess that's what girls do, huh?"

Mrs. Walsh looked troubled. "Mark, why do you ask such a question so long after your mother died? Is something wrong in your family? Brit tells me you seem to have some problems," she asked.

"No," Mark said, embarrassed at the woman's insight. "It's just that I wanted to know more about my mom. It's, you know, nice to know they were happy . . . my parents . . . "

"Well," Mrs. Walsh said, "all I can say is, when we were together, your mother never complained about your father to me. I'd gripe about my Roy, but she never would. You needn't worry that your mother wasn't happy, Mark. It was a very good marriage. It's just so sad, so terribly sad that she had that stupid accident. But things happen for a reason. We just don't understand the reasons, but we have to do the best we can in the here and now . . . "

Mrs. Walsh drove to her house with Mark and gave him her own personal scrapbook. It contained pictures of herself and Mark's mom and some of their other friends. She told Mark to keep it as long as he liked. Then Mrs. Walsh drove Mark to his grandparents' home and waved good-bye.

Mark was grateful for the time he spent with her. She seemed to be a very nice person. But he wasn't convinced that his mom was happy in her marriage. How could she have been when they were arguing so violently that night? There must have been deep, terrible problems. Maybe his mom was just too proud to share them, even with her closest friend.

Mark went to his room at his grandparents' house and looked at the scrapbook. There were pictures of a teenage Belle Lee playing in the snow with her friends. Pictures of her at an amusement park. The best picture was of her stuffing cake in another girl's face. There were also pictures of the Fitch Antique Cars store with a bunch of students from Lincoln High posing by the old cars and hot rods.

Mark found a very cute picture of his mother in shorts. She was perched on the hood of a hot rod. Reggie was leaning on the front of the car. Mark lifted the picture out of the plastic film and noticed handwriting on the back.

"Reggie, whom I will always love, Belle Lee."

Mark stared at the picture. They looked so good together, his mom and Reggie.

As he was looking, his grandpa appeared peering over his shoulder.

"Watcha got there?" he asked.

"Some pictures of Mom and her friends. I visited with Brit Walsh's mom today. She let me look at her scrapbook. I really like these pictures of Mom. They're . . . nice," Mark said, a lump in his throat.

His grandpa fell silent. "Belle's best friend was Joanna Stevens. What a lot of fun those little girls had. Got into more scrapes, but you couldn't even be really mad at either one of them. Too lovable they were . . . " his grandpa said, gently lifting one of the pictures up and staring at it. "It tore the heart right out of me when we lost her. I couldn't believe it, boy. My precious little girl." His voice was thick and sad.

"I didn't want to make you feel bad, Grandpa," Mark said. "I just don't have many pictures of Mom, and I wanted to see a few. Especially showing her so happy."

His grandpa mussed his hair in a loving way. "Don't you worry. You're all right. I understand how you feel. Happy little girl, wasn't she? Look at that smile," he said, his eyes bright with tears even when his lips smiled.

Then he stopped smiling.

"I accepted the accident. I took it for what it looked like on the face of it. But I never did like your father. Lord forgive me, but it's the truth. And now that we know he lied about that night, I'd like to take the man and break him in two. I won't, of course, but I feel a fierce hatred inside me."

"Grandpa, I'm sorry I caused trouble like this," Mark said.

"It wasn't your doing, boy. It was his. It grinds me that all these years he had us believing they didn't argue, that they got along fine and he treated her like a queen. He swore he never once raised his voice to her, and like fools we believed it." Mark's grandpa's jaw tightened and then he said, "Makes me wonder if maybe she didn't die by accident at all."

Mark turned icy cold. The same suspicion had been in his heart all these years. It scarred his tormented memory and gave him no peace. But hearing his grandpa actually say it was horrifying in a new and painful way. It made it more real.

"Mark, I'm going to ask you something," his grandpa said, "and I want you to think hard before you answer."

"Okay," Mark said.

"Are you one hundred percent sure that you heard the arguing that night? There's not even an outside chance that it could have been a nightmare? Or the TV? Or anything else but what you said?" his grandpa asked.

"Grandpa, I heard those voices, yelling and screaming. I'd never heard anything like it before. I cried. I made my pillow wet from crying. I had never heard something like that before, and I was so scared. I thought it was the end of the world or something. I tried to stuff part of the blanket in my ears, but I couldn't stop the noises. Then I heard the thump, thump on the stairs, like something bouncing. Later on I knew what it was," Mark said.

"Oh my," his grandpa groaned.

"Grandpa, as awful as it was, I might have forgotten about it in the morning if Mom hadn't been . . . gone. It got fixed in my mind because I never saw Mom again," Mark said.

"That dirty little creep," his grandpa said in a bitter voice. "All this time he hid what happened. He hid the truth. Made it seem like he came home to find her lying there. And he'd been there all through it. And he got away with it. If only someone else had seen or heard something that night. It's not too late to bring murder charges, you know. There's no statute of limitations on murder . . . "

Mark felt his world crumbling even more beneath his feet, like the earth itself was giving way, flinging him into chaos.

He had caused all this. If he had kept his mouth shut none of this would be happening now. But he couldn't be silent anymore . . . *he couldn't.*

"Grandpa, there's a Mrs. Kennerly who lived next door. She was there the night

Mom . . . died," Mark said in a dull, sad voice. "Maybe she's still living. Maybe she'd remember something."

10 MARK AND HIS grandfather drove over to the Victorian house where he had lived before his mother died. The man Mark had talked to earlier gave them Mrs. Kennerly's address at an assisted living facility.

"Not good," Mark's grandpa said. "She probably doesn't remember a whole lot anymore."

They drove to the Olive View Gardens and found Mrs. Kennerly in a tidy one-bedroom apartment. She was 85 and seemed glad to have visitors of any kind. "Oh, yes, I remember that young couple who lived next door," she said. "The girl was such a pretty, cheerful little thing. Always chatting with me. She'd go to the store, buy some strawberries, and bring me some too. That's how she was. The husband wasn't around much. He worked at some lab. My husband and I used to wonder how such a vivacious girl was getting along with that mousy little man."

"Do you remember the night Mrs. Ryder died?" Mark's grandpa asked. His brow was furrowed with pain.

"Oh, yes. It was the most dramatic thing that ever happened on our street. We were all shocked. Police, paramedics were all over the place. It was awful," Mrs. Kennerly said.

"Did you hear anything unusual at the house that night?" Mark's grandpa asked.

"Well, we had the television on. My hearing wasn't very good, anyway. I never heard very much. The police asked me a lot of questions . . . but I couldn't help them. I think they suspected something fishy over there, but nothing ever came of it. My granddaughter was staying with me that week. She was just 11. Nobody questioned her. I didn't want her mixed up in something sordid . . . " Mrs. Kennerly said.

"Do you think she might have heard something?" Mark's grandpa asked.

"I do recall she said something about hearing an argument next door . . . I'm not sure though. I didn't want her questioned.

She was such a sensitive little girl," Mrs. Kennerly said.

In 20 minutes, Mark and his grandfather were driving to an apartment near downtown where Allison Kennerly lived. Her grandmother had given them the address.

"This is probably a complete wild-goose chase," Mark's grandpa commented, "but it's worth a try."

"Yeah," Mark said. "But Mrs. Kennerly did say the girl heard an argument. I mean, until now, it's just been what *I* remembered. You don't know what it means to me to know that somebody else heard the same thing!"

Allison was a computer specialist who lived in a high-rise condo. She welcomed Mark and his grandpa. Her grandmother had called her to tell her they were coming.

"I guess you want to know about that night 12 years ago," she said. "Well, I was staying with Gram the first time ever. It was so boring until that night. All of a sudden I hear this terrible fighting next door. I mean, my own parents scrapped a lot, but nothing like this. I thought it was something on TV. Then I opened my window and looked out, and I could hear them clearly. He was cursing at her. It was so ugly."

Mark saw the anguish grow in his grandfather's face. He was wincing at the thought of what his precious daughter must have gone through that last night of her life. Mark was thinking the same thing. It must have been an awful marriage.

Allison continued, "Then, all of a sudden it got quiet, and I thought I'd get some sleep. I did see the husband come dashing out the front door. Man, was he going fast. He ran to a hot rod parked on the corner, and he took off like a race car driver. I thought he'd decided to leave his wife for good. I was glad too. Nobody should have to live like that."

"And then?" Mark's grandpa prodded.

"Well, then something weird happened. Another car pulled up. This little guy went to the door . . . he went right in because the door was sort of standing open. Maybe he was another neighbor, and he heard the fighting too, and he was worried about the woman. Anyway, he called the police I guess because the whole night filled with red lights and sirens. I saw the paramedic guys carry the woman out. I'd never seen her before, but Gram said it was the wife. You could tell she was in bad shape. Right away I thought the husband beat her up or something, and that's why he ran off. He knew he'd hurt her bad. Gram wouldn't let me talk to the police, though. She called my parents and rushed me home."

Mark and his grandfather looked at the girl as she finished her story. Their minds were spinning wildly.

"There was an article in the paper about it, and it said the husband came home from work and found his wife dead. What a crock! I mean, I heard them fighting . . . I told my parents, but they said I was just a crazy kid and I needn't get mixed up in it. My dad said I probably didn't know what I was looking at anyway," Allison said, her face showing disgust. "I should have told somebody, though. I mean, what a bully that husband was. Gram said the wife was a little thing, and here's this big, tall guy, he must've been over six foot or something . . . cursing at her and then maybe hurting her."

"Six foot?" Mark repeated. "My dad's not six feet tall." Mark turned and looked at his grandpa. "Are you thinking what I'm thinking?"

"Yep," his grandpa replied.

"Thanks for your time. We've got all the information we need." The two men shook hands with Allison then dashed out to the car.

When Mark and his grandfather were back in the car, Mark said, "Grandpa, the guy Allison saw running from the house after the fighting was *tall*. He was a big guy, Grandpa . . ."

"I heard," his grandpa said tensely. His breath came in excited gasps. "That girl just assumed the guy running from the house was the husband. She'd never seen your mother or father before! But there was someone else in that house that night."

Mark was drenched in perspiration.

"Grandpa! That's why my dad sounded so strange! I thought he sounded different and I figured it was because I'd never heard him scream and holler before . . . but it wasn't my dad!" Mark said.

"And the little guy the girl saw driving up," his grandpa continued, "the one she thought was a neighbor . . . that was your father coming home from work just like he has been saying all along . . . "

"But Grandpa, who could the other guy have been? My mom wouldn't have ever let a stranger in," Mark said.

Mark's grandpa's eyes narrowed. "Wasn't a stranger. It was a guy who drove a hot rod. A big guy. Had to be Reggie Fitch. Belle Lee used to tell me how he'd come around begging her to run off with him. Belle was so kindhearted. She'd take time to make him coffee and talk to him. I told her she was a married woman, and it wasn't right for an old boyfriend to be coming around. She'd say she still felt guilty for dumping him. She felt sorry for him. Maybe she was flattered that he still loved her so much. But I guess that night she decided to end it for good."

They went to Fitch's Antique Cars. Reggie wasn't there, but his father was. Mark's grandfather recognized the elder Fitch right away. "We want to talk to Reggie," Mark's grandpa said.

"That's a tall order," Joe Fitch answered.

"Isn't he around?" Mark's grandpa demanded. "We need to know where he is, Mr. Fitch."

Joe Fitch blinked as he looked at Mark's grandpa. "Don't I know you?" he asked.

"Yeah, I'm Belle Lee Crosley's father. My daughter and a lot of the kids from Lincoln High hung out here in the old days," Mark's grandpa said.

"Yeah, that's right. Our kids dated, didn't they?" Mr. Fitch said.

"Where's Reggie?" Mark's grandpa demanded again.

"Hasn't been around for 12 years, brother," Mr. Fitch said. "That's when we buried him."

Mr. Fitch led Mark and his grandfather into the shop. He poured them each a cup of black coffee from a rusty pot. Mark's grandpa had said the antique car and hot rod shop was a popular hangout, full of life. But now cobwebs circled the tired old cars. They were no longer classic cars. They were all junk now. And nobody hung around anymore except scavengers looking for parts.

"Reggie's life went downhill a long time ago. He got obsessed with your daughter. I kept telling him to forget about her, but he wouldn't. All the time she was dating that other guy, he'd be calling her. And then when she got married, he didn't stop. He'd find out when her husband would be gone, and he'd go over there and try to get her to come away with him. Well, that one night he went over there. I didn't know anything about it until it was all over . . . he was much different after that. The hope had gone out of him. He started drinking heavily. He didn't want to do anything or go anywhere. He was haunted by something . . . "

"Are you talking about the night my daughter died?" Mark's grandpa asked.

"I read in the paper that she'd died. I thought maybe he could finally forget her.

I thought he could get on with his life. But then he told me what had happened. He told me Belle Lee said she loved her husband and she would always love him, and Reggie just had to go. My son said he went sort of crazy. He said the girl ran up the stairs, and he ran after her. They struggled at the top of the stairs. She fell.

"After that happened, his life took a turn for the worst. One night he was out driving in the desert. Missed a curve. When they found him in the gully he'd been dead for five days," Mr. Fitch said.

Mark and his father said nothing as they drove to the apartment where Mark used to live with his father. When they got there, the place was semi-dark. They had to ring the bell five times to rouse Mark's father.

"Dad," Mark said. "We found the truth!"

His dad just stood there, transfixed.

Taking turns, Mark and his grandfather told the whole tragic story. When they had finished, Mark's grandpa apologized. Harry looked like a man emerging from a trauma. "I thought I'd lost everything," he said. "I'd already lost my Belle Lee, the only woman I've ever loved, and then my boy. It was all I had left. My boy. And he was gone. I didn't think I could make it. I don't think I cared anymore if I did or not."

Mark grabbed his father and hugged him. It was the first time he had been in his father's arms since he was four. "I love you, Dad," Mark whispered. Tears streamed down his face.

"Love you, too, boy," his father said.

It would be the first time in 12 years that Mark could believe those words.